The Little Troll

Story by Thomas Berger
Illustrated by Ronald Heuninck

Based on a folk-tale by Jeanna Oterdahl

Floris Books

Deep in the forest among stunted fir-trees and boggy woodland lakes, there lived a little troll and his friends. Short and squat with matted hair and small red-rimmed eyes, the little troll was very ugly to look at.

The trolls loved storms and wind best of all! They hissed and howled with the roaring wind and rain.

Trolls hate things to be sunny and light and good. Above all, they hate human beings because of their fine upright walk and their clear eyes.

But our little troll was strangely different from the rest. He liked humans! Deep in his little troll-heart, he wished he was like a human himself. Humans were straight and tall, while trolls were short and squat. Humans had fine voices. Trolls spoke roughly and coarsely.

But of course he could say nothing of this to his troll friends. So he howled and hissed with the others although he didn't really enjoy it.

Often the little troll climbed among the gigantic mossy stones and peered along paths just to see if he could catch sight of a human.

If he was lucky, a charcoal-burner might come along, or a wood-cutter, or an old woman gathering sticks, or some children looking for berries or mushrooms.

One night in deep winter, a noise drew him close to the village where the humans lived. From the village there came a wonderful sound. It was the ringing of the church bells.

In the starlight he crept down the hill, nearer and nearer, like a little fearful shadow. He tried to look through the church windows which were all iced and frosted over. He could not see much, but he thought he glimpsed a face shining peacefully in candlelight.

Something wonderful was going on in there. He did not understand why, but from his ugly little eyes tears rolled down and froze in the snow.

Lonely and sad, he slipped back into the forest. That night he howled in the dark like all the other trolls.

One day he followed an old charcoal-burner and his grandson back to their hut at the edge of the forest. He crouched outside the window, peeped in and listened to them talking.

The charcoal-burner was cutting thick slices of bread for their supper.

"If you want to be a real man," he was saying to the boy, "you must learn to think of others more than yourself. If you don't help and serve others, you're nothing better than a troll."

Outside, the little troll pricked up his hairy ears. So that was the difference between trolls and humans. To be a real human being, you had to help others!

He crept away thinking, who should he help? Not his troll-friends! They would soon send him packing. He would try to help the animals in the forest and, yes, above all, he would help the human beings themselves!

The little troll set about helping in the only way he knew. One day he saw three children coming into the forest to gather blueberries. They put a basket on the ground to fill.

When the children were not looking, the little troll crept up and soon filled the basket with the fattest blueberries he could find. The children were amazed to discover the basket full.

"Someone has been helping us," cried the eldest child. "Thank you, whoever you are!"

"Thank you, thank you!" cried the others. And the little troll, hiding again between the stones, was happier than he had ever been. No one had ever said thank-you to him before.

From then on people from the village started to find it lucky to go up into the forest. Everyone who had work to do there, received some kind of help. The more the little troll learned to help, the more skilful he became and the more he enjoyed doing it. But he never dared to show himself to the human beings.

But at home in the depths of the forest, things were not going well for him. The other trolls could smell that something was wrong.

"What's the matter with you?" they cried. "You're growing horribly tall! You're getting bigger than a troll ought to be. You're getting less hairy. You almost look like a human being! Ugh!"

And they started to pinch him and push him around.

A girl started to come to the forest on her own. She came to pick flowers, berries or mushrooms. She always sang as she worked and the troll thought her voice was even more beautiful than the church bells.

The troll helped her eagerly. Her basket was filled in moments with the choicest things he could find for her. The girl never went without calling out a thank-you. Often she left part of her midday meal as a return gift.

Although there were dangers in the forest, no harm ever came to the girl. Once a bear wandering too close had suddenly trotted off in another direction. Another time, a falling tree was hurled aside and she was unhurt.

But the girl never caught a glimpse of her helper.

One autumn day the girl came to the forest for the last time before winter. Her basket was soon filled with snow-white mushrooms gathered by her invisible helper.

"Dear helper, whoever you are," she said, "why don't you show yourself?"

But the troll, afraid that his ugliness would scare her, didn't dare come out .

"Tell me what I can give you in return," said the girl. "Ask me for anything."

Then a whisper came from somewhere, she didn't know where: "On Christmas Day, breathe on the frosted window of the church till the ice melts."

"That's a strange request," thought the girl, but she said: "Yes, if that's all you want, it's easily done. But if we should ever meet, I'd like to have some way of knowing you. Take my little silver cross and wear it. It will bring you luck."

The troll watched till the girl departed through the trees. Then he came out and took the gift that she had left on a rock.

It was a poor worn cross of thin silver, but for the little troll it was the greatest treasure he had ever possessed. He wore the cross round his neck, tucked in carefully under his fur coat.

From that day on his desire to be human became even greater and he spent all his time helping and serving others. Whenever he was not helping people, he looked after the animals, large and small.

Slowly — so slowly that he didn't even notice — his body grew straighter and straighter. His skin became less hairy and his voice smoother and sweeter for the animals to hear.

The troll had now changed completely and the other trolls pestered him more and more.

"You aren't like a troll any more!" they roared. "You're starting to look like a human! Ugh! Away with you! You don't belong here any more!"

So saying, they drove him away. Alone and unhappy, he wandered in the forest. He didn't belong anywhere. He was no longer a troll, but he wasn't human either. As a troll, he had not felt the cold, but now he froze and shivered. Only from the silver cross on his breast, there came a gentle warmth. He thought he could bear anything if only he were human. Had all his helping been for nothing? He felt cold, exhausted and lost.

Suddenly a distant sound reached his ears.
Without realizing, he had come nearer and nearer to
the village. It was the church bells, ringing for
Christmas Day. He stumbled on towards the sound.

Soon in the distance he could see the church-goers arriving on sledges, their lamps flickering in the half-light. Before long they had all gone into the church and closed the doors. The little troll walked slowly towards the frosted glow of the church windows.

Inside the church, as she had promised, the girl was breathing on the window. The ice lay in thick sparkling leaves over the panes. But her breath did not melt it and she laid her warm cheek against the icy glass.

"What are you doing there, child?" chided her mother.

"I'm letting the Christmas light shine out for someone outside, mother," replied the girl.

Slowly the last ice melted and ran down the pane. She saw a face pressed close and two dark eyes full of longing. A hand held up the silver cross.

"Welcome, dweller of the woods," she whispered.